To Taylar
with lots of love from Na
Gina Thompson.
x

The Boy who Tried to Catch the Sun

The Boy who Tried
to
Catch the Sun

Gina Thompson

ATHENA PRESS
LONDON

THE BOY WHO TRIED TO CATCH THE SUN
Copyright © Gina Thompson 2008

All Rights Reserved

No part of this book may be reproduced in any form
by photocopying or by any electronic or mechanical means,
including information storage or retrieval systems,
without permission in writing from both the copyright
owner and the publisher of this book.

ISBN 978 1 84748 388 1

First published 2008
ATHENA PRESS
Queen's House, 2 Holly Road
Twickenham TW1 4EG
United Kingdom

Printed for Athena Press

One day, a boy called
Jonathan Lindow

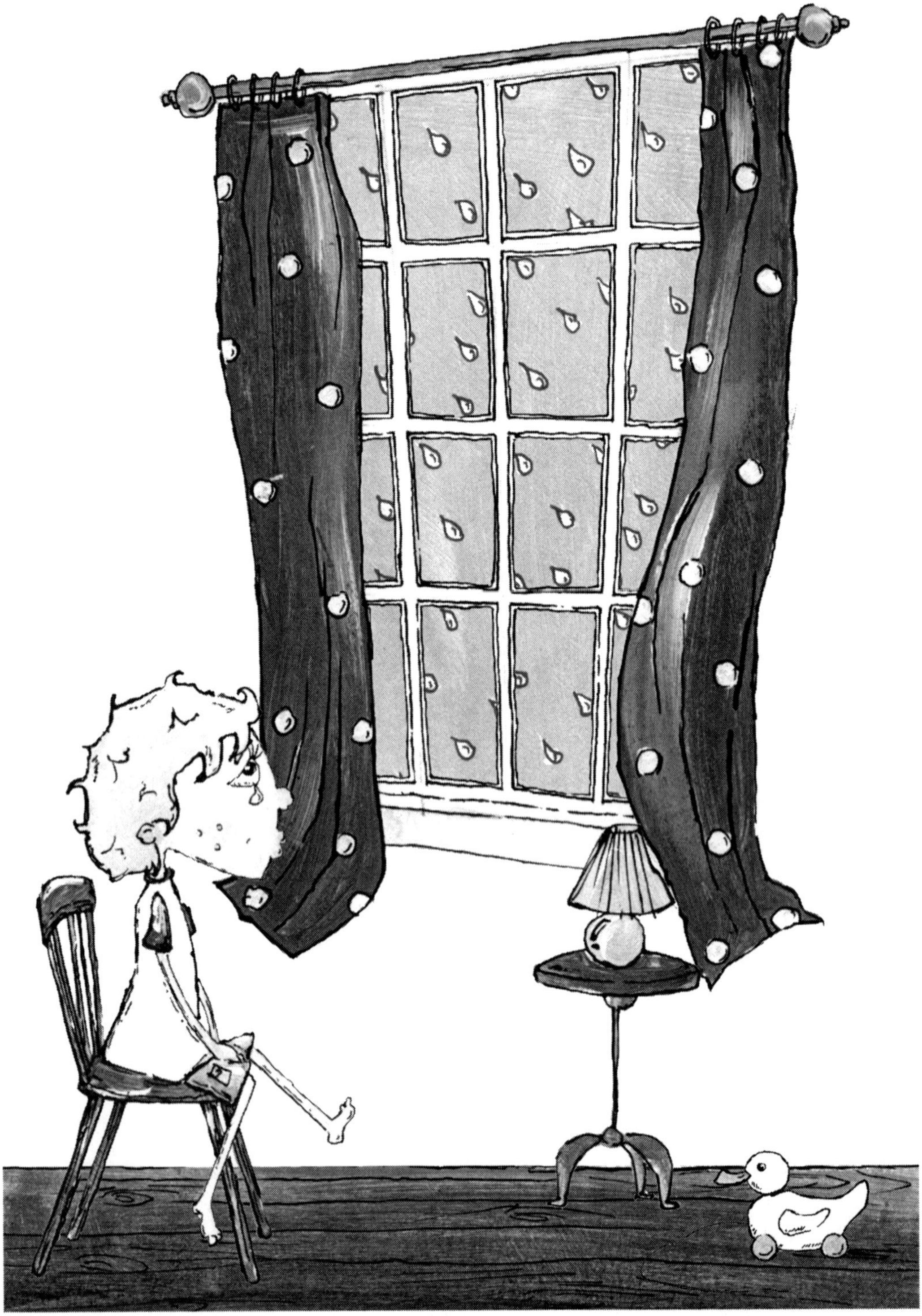

sat watching the rain beating down on the window.

'Oh, isn't it miserable,' Jonathan cried.

'It's raining so hard that I can't play outside.'

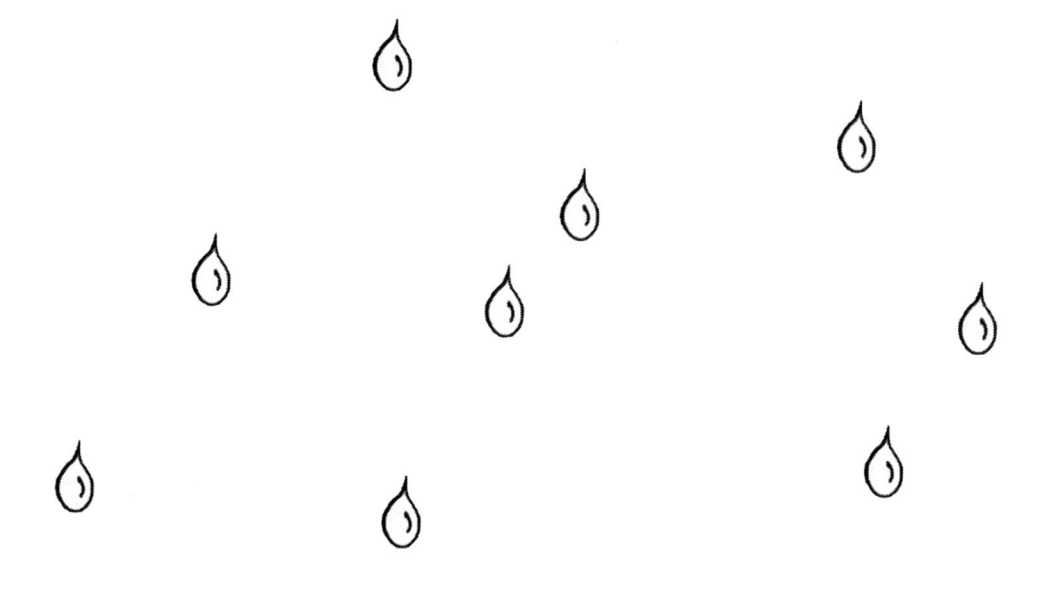

He looked at his toys spread over the floor,

but nothing amused him,
                        it was all such a bore.

To think yesterday morning was
sunny and hot,

and he'd played in the garden and
laughed such a lot.

He sat and he thought,
did Jonathan Lindow,

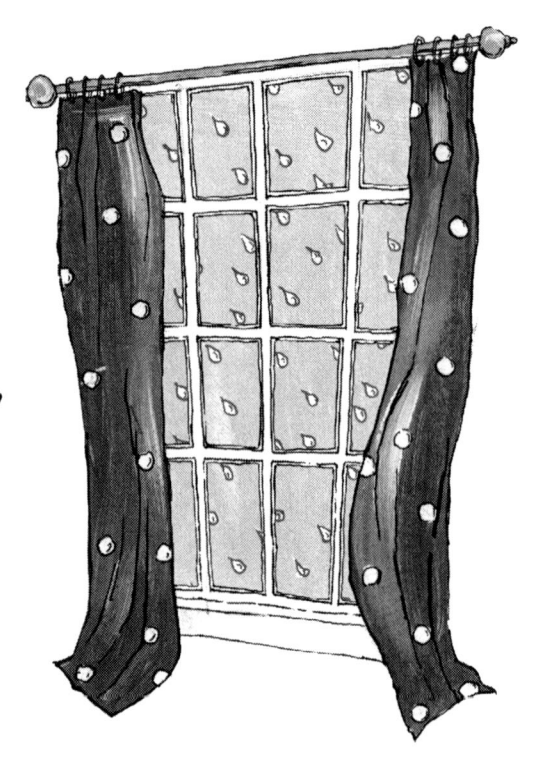

he thought such a lot
as he sat by the window.

'If only I'd saved some of yesterday's sun,

I'd be out there right now having so much
good fun.'

'The next time the sun comes shining all day,

I'll catch some and keep it for the next rainy day.

Then all I need do is to let the sun out,

and my problems are solved without any doubt!"

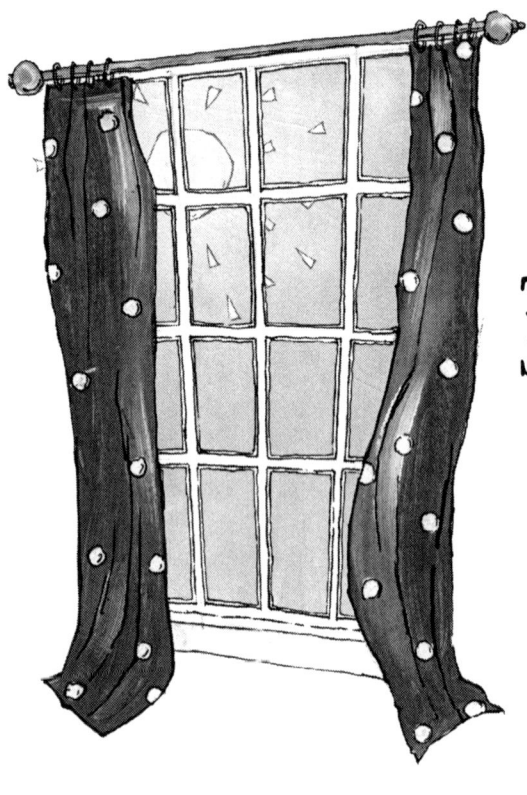

The next day, when Jonathan got out of bed,

he ran to the window and joyfully said,

'The sun! It is shining!
Oh, what a good day,

I'll be quick with my breakfast
and go out to play.'

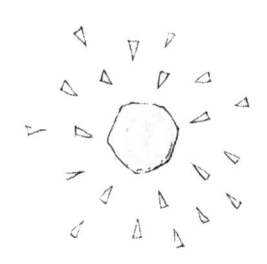

But thinking of yesterday's miserable rain,

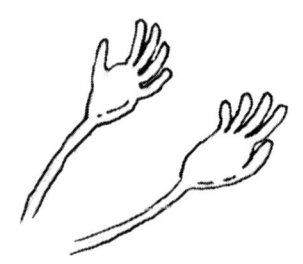

of catching some sunshine he thought once again.

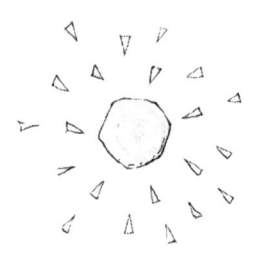

'Yes! That's what I'll do
 and I'll do it right now.

I'll go catching sunshine! The problem is...
How?'

19

'A net! That will do it! The way I catch fish.
I'll scoop up some sunshine to save in a dish!'

He scooped and he scooped at the sun in the sky,

but couldn't catch sunshine,
             although he did try.

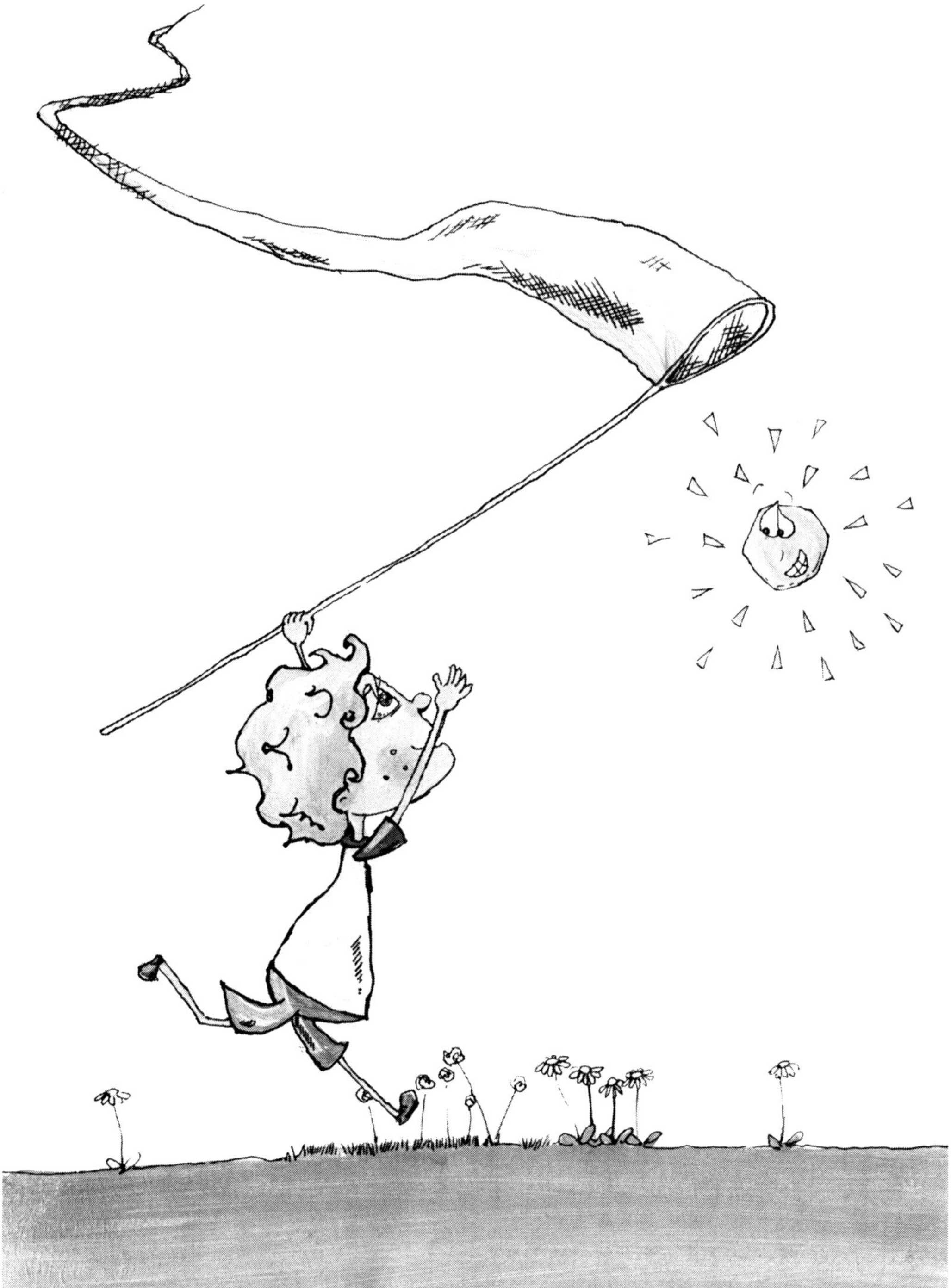

'The sun must escape through the holes in this net. I'll try something else, I won't give up yet.'

He next brought a blanket and threw it right over

the sunshine that lay on the daisies and clover.

He peeked under the blanket and cried in dismay,

'I either have missed it or it got away.

Now what can I use? An old biscuit tin!

I saw one last night by the side of the bin.'

He picked up the tin and opened it up,

then went in his house and took out a cup.

He cupped at the sky and tipped it in the tin,

but not a thing happened, nothing went in.

He tried yet again with a pan and a jar, a bag, then a box that came with his toy car.

He swept and he swooped and he looked with a frown,

but nothing would catch
the sun shining down.

Jonathan sighed,
'I just cannot do it,

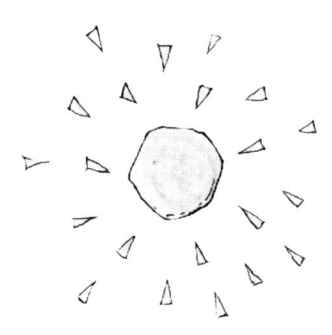

whatever I try, the sun just goes through it.

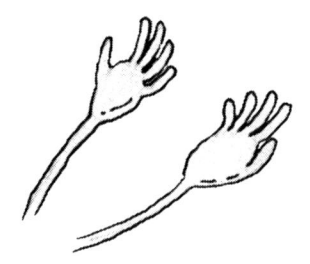

This catching the sun is a difficult task.

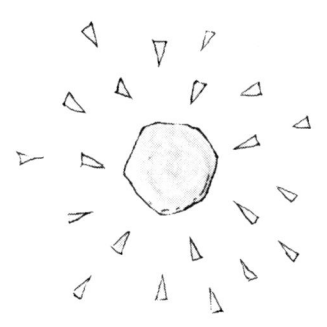

I need some advice - but who can I ask?'

He went to the wise owl perched up in a tree

and shouted to him,
'Could you please help me?

I need some advice
and I've come to ask you.'

'Of course,' said the owl
and down he flew.

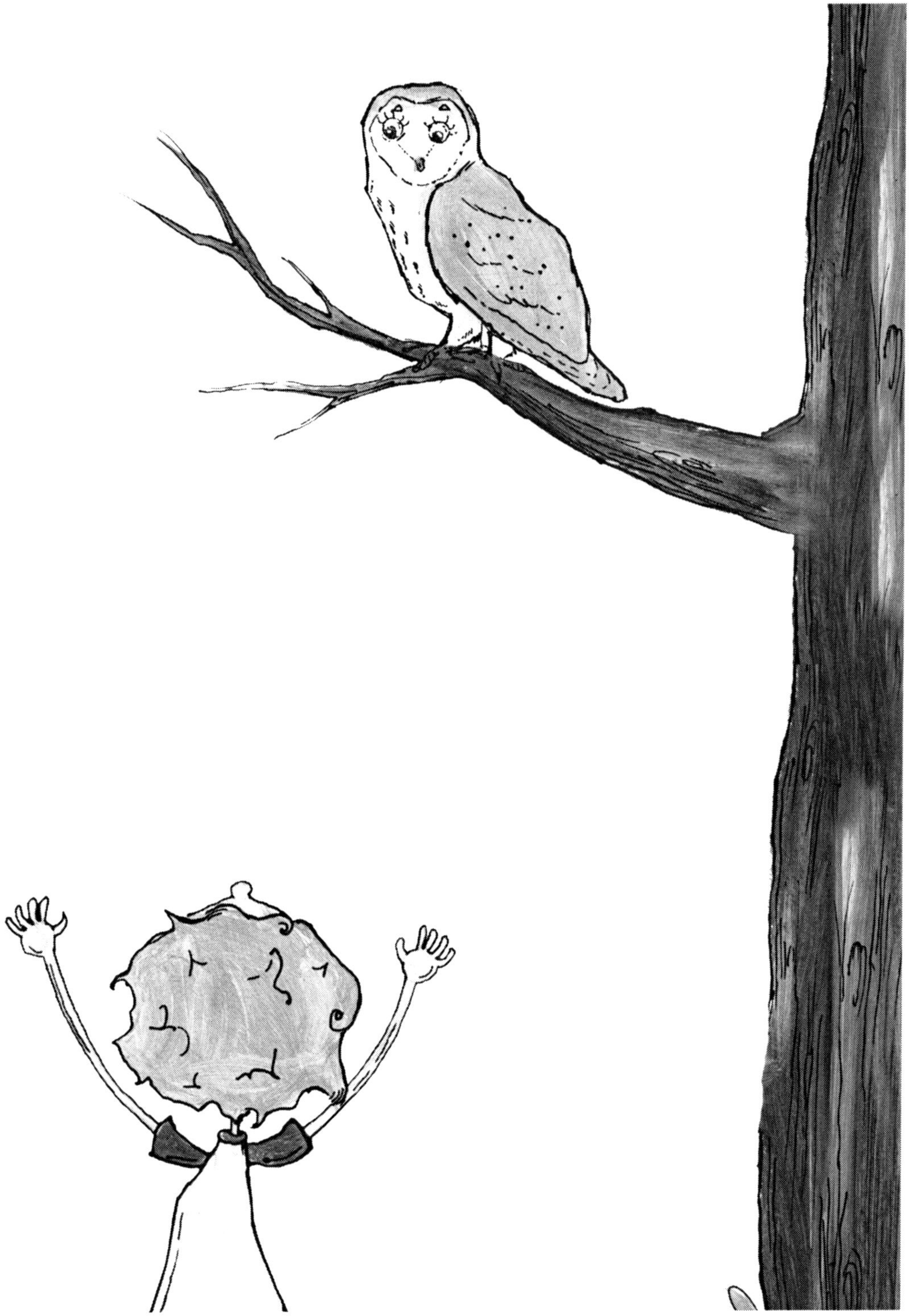

Owl fluttered around, then perched on a bough.

'Please, where I can catch some sunshine - and how?'

Jonathan asked meekly.

The wise owl thought long.

'You can't catch the sunshine.
To try would be wrong.

'The sun in the sky is like the wind in a tree:

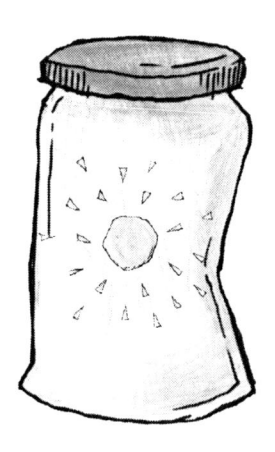

The wind you can feel and the sun you can see;

but neither one can be put in a jar,

no matter how quick or how clever you are.

'Imagine if you made the sun shine each day,

the flowers and plants would soon wither away.

So sometimes the rain comes to
wet all the ground,

to water the plants and
    to wash all around.

'So the sun must be free to shine in the sky

or to hide in the clouds when
the ground is too dry.'

Jonathan listened to the great wise old bird

and thought very deeply about what he'd heard.

'I've been very selfish,' Jonathan said sadly.

'Just thinking of ME, I've behaved very badly.

In future, when the rain comes and I can't play,

I'll simply just wait for the next sunny day!'

This is the third book by GINA THOMPSON, who started writing stories for her own children when they were young. She continues to use her own stories in her work with vulnerable children and uses rhyme to communicate feelings and emotions. She lives and works in Keighley, West Yorkshire.

Printed in the United Kingdom
by Lightning Source UK Ltd.
132878UK00001B/223-230/P